DEATH

& Sparkles 1

by Rob Justus

chronicle books · san francisco

Death
doesn't
care.

Big, short,

tall,

small.

Young... Two-legged...

beep, beep

quack

and old. or eight.

One fatal touch from

the cold hand of Death . . .

Death can be many things ...

a sad experience,

Nothing will ever be the same.

a sigh of relief,
He's no longer suffering.

a celebration of life.
He was truly loved.

One thing for sure—death is not easy.

It's a junk job.

How can you have friends . . .

when all you touch . . .

withers and dies?

Okay. Deal's a deal.
Spit it out.

REALLY?!
Where do we
even begin?

I guess I'll start at the beginning. We're actually not human; we're a reptilian alien race from billions of light-years away. It is our mission to travel across the universe to help young planets grow into responsible cosmic citizens. We've lived among humanity for centuries, helping the people of the world grow and prosper. Great inventions that everyone takes for granted, we probably had a hand in helping humans "discover." That said . . . things haven't really gone according to plan. For as much as we've helped humanity, humans have actually taken a lot of our technology and turned it against themselves and this planet. So much so that the planet is dying, and we're doing our ned. these potentially catastrophic we're here to see you. t ca tention! And you have all the atten g you could spread the d t Lizard People

Hrmm.

From there we can m___ the two techn___gies in ___ sim-ple process ___at we ___efer___ as S___ Proto W___e Sy___ osi___ the ___vels ___ ar___ ___n th___ used ___ har___

Hey there, friend. Selling something to Sparkles without his manager?

Well, actually we were seeing if Sparkles could help us spread the word of our alien lizard technology to help save your planet from harmful climate change. It's really quite ingenious—

That's great and all, but I'm going to give you some advice . . .

I wish I had
a cupcake.

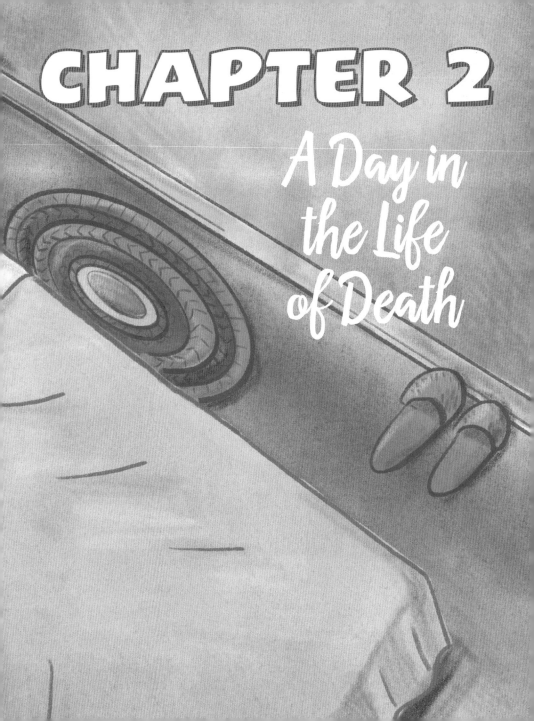

CHAPTER 2

A Day in the Life of Death

click

48

CHAPTER 4

NEWS FLASH

Sparkles, the last unicorn, is dead.

Set to release his highly anticipated designer sock
line today, Sparkles tragically passed away performing
his most elaborate promotional stunt yet,
dubbed the Office Tower Sock Shower!

In what seemed to be a tragic chariot malfunction, Sparkles plunged three hundred stories, crashing in a fiery wreck—showering devoted fans with his colorful, high-quality cotton socks. Which are now selling for record prices online.

The world will be a less—

—aherm—
I told myself I wasn't going to cry—
herm.

The world will be a darker place without Sparkles's sunshine and SUPER expensive merchandise enlightening our lives.

Thankfully, Sparkle Corp, Sparkles's management company, is offering this commemorative coupon—when you purchase ten pairs of socks, you'll receive the eleventh for five percent off when you use the code.

#SparklesIsSuperDead

Now, that's a deal! And just how Sparkles —*sniff*— would've wanted it.

CHAPTER 4 AND A HALF

A Second Chance

Let us take a moment to remember all the joy that Sparkles, the last unicorn, brought to this planet.

Even though he was a total jerk to us in real life.

But in this time of tragedy . . .

COMES OPPORTUNITY!

Now is our time to shine!

With Sparkles gone, the humans will no longer be distracted by shiny trinkets.

85

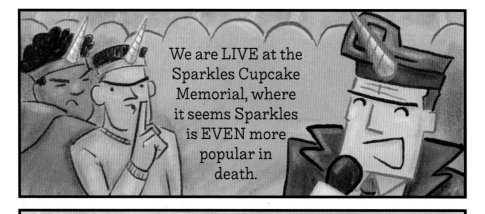

We are LIVE at the Sparkles Cupcake Memorial, where it seems Sparkles is EVEN more popular in death.

That's right, Barry! Thousands here, millions around the world are mourning everyone's favorite bestie, Sparkles.

I can't believe this is happening. Just yesterday I was eating Sparkle-O's cereal and wearing my favorite unicorn slippers, and now he's gone!

Y'know, I used to be kinda over Sparkles, y'know. I mean his face is everywhere, y'know. But now that he's gone, I really miss him, y'know.

CHAPTER 6
Come Toward the Light

SPARKLES!

Who said that? Where am I? Am I dead?

You are neither alive nor dead. You are in the void. The passage before paradise.

That explains the floating . . .

GIMME!
GIMME!
GIMME!

I can't
reach it!

That is because your
time has not come yet.

Oh, yeah? Who says so?

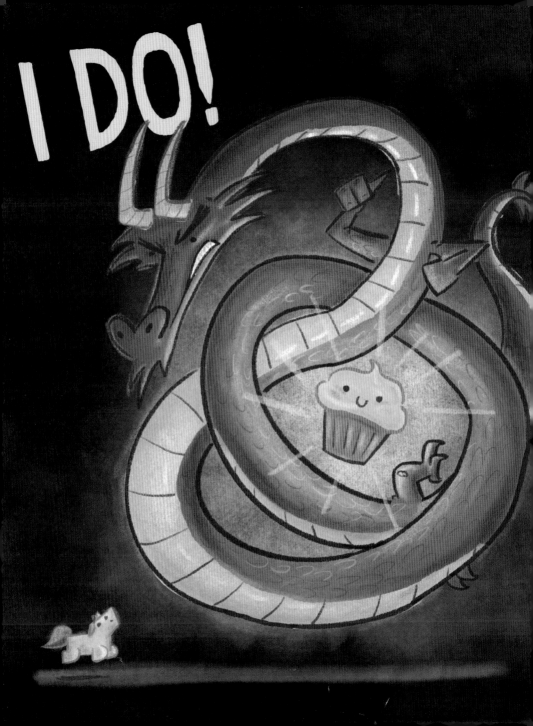

There is much more
work to be done
before you are
allowed into paradise.

What do you know?
All I've ever done is work.
I just finished recording my
fourth Christmas album
and consulted on my line
of Sparkles hair plugs.

Not to mention all the
kids I cheer up at birthday
parties, bar mitzvahs,
strawberry socials, high
teas. The list goes on!

Listen closely.

You are the last of the unicorns.

A noble animal.

For eons, unicorns used their magic to guard against the planet's greatest threat . . .

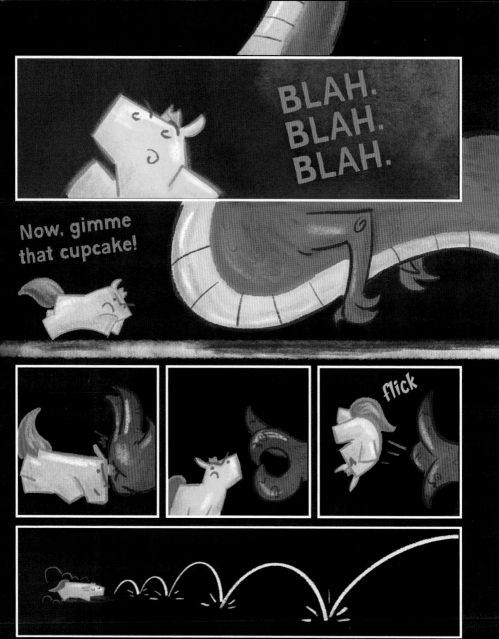

Sparkles, you have been wasting your life! You are not worthy of the giant cupcake yet. Change your ways, unlock your TRUE potential, or **FACE THE CONSEQUENCES!**

Oh, yeah? What might that be? Another reality TV series?!

Look deep inside your soul and you will find the answer.

CHAPTER 7
An Ugly Start to a Beautiful Friendship

YES!
I fell on it!

No, it's stuck!
Like, REALLY stuck!

It hurts so bad.

Where am I?
What's going on?
Am I upside down?

Uhhhhhh . . . Why are
you alive???
I touched you.
You should be dead.

I don't wanna
die again!

CHAPTER 7 ⅓

Friends in Need

ARRRRRRRRGH!

Stupid, stupid humans!

We did everything that Mom and Dad and the elders told us to. We were polite and kind. We dressed smart. We didn't scare them with our lizard ways.

We're the freaking NICE GUYS! Amiright?
What's wrong with this planet of fools?

How long do we have to go until we get their attention? How many millennia?!
We show them how to make electricity.
We give them cool computers.
Teach them about math. We even showed them the wheel!

The wheel, people!

Here we are, trying to save THEIR crummy planet! And they don't even care!

All they want is sparkles and bonbons.
We're just a bunch of lizard failures.

Ahem.

CRACK!

Ouch.

Nope.
It didn't work.

Hehe!

Aren't you
some sort of
ALL-powerful
magical unicorn?

Okay. Seriously.
Let's put our heads
together and find
a way out of this
situation.

I got nothing . . .

Me neither . . .

Sure is a nice sunset, at least . . .

Honestly, killing
people isn't all it's
cracked up to be.

No way!

Way.

And it's not really
killing. It's more
CLAIMING A
PERSON'S SOUL.
There's a lot of little rules
and stuff. Like, I have to
touch someone in order
to claim them. Shells
and, I guess, horns don't
respond to my powers.
It's weird. I don't make
up the rules. So I'm
not sure why you keep
coming back?

I know why! It's because
I'm not worthy of the giant
cupcake, right?

Ummmmmmmm . . .
yeah, I've never heard
about this cupcake thing.

So what happens
if you don't
claim a soul?

Oh, you can still die!
Your soul, however,
is just kinda stuck.

Huh? What does
that mean?

You're in limbo. You
have no body, but
the soul is still here.
Trapped. Kinda like a
ghost . . . well, I guess,
exactly like a ghost.

That doesn't
sound so cool.

Yeah . . . Death can be
messy . . . But I guess
someone has to do this
dirty work.

Why?

It's my job.
I've just done
it for so long . . .

Why not just quit?
Then we could
play X-tendo all day!

Ha! Just quit!
Huh . . . Noooooo,
I couldn't do that!

Sometimes I wish I could quit *my* job.

I never really have any days off.
I'm always being told where to be and what
to do. I wouldn't have done that crazy stunt
if my manager didn't make me do it.

I mean, it's nice having the whole entire
world love me and want to be my friend, but
some days I kinda just wish I could sit down
and read a book, and not have my photo
taken, or be asked for candy, or have fans
rubbing my horn or trying to tickle
rainbows out of me.

I wish someone would
tickle rainbows out of me.

There's so much I'd like to
try but will never be able
to do. Play tag. Slap some
fives. Give fist bumps . . .
or even just get a hug.

You're the first thing that can touch
me without dying, and frankly, this
is not how I thought it'd turn out.

I mean your horn really, really, really
hurts. Like, so bad. It is SO sharp.

I could really go for some
cupcakes about now.

I've never had a cupcake before.
Are they any good?

Whaaaaaat?
You've never had a cupcake before?

D, if we ever get off this cliff,
I'll totally introduce you to cupcakes.

They alone make life worth living.

Uh-oh . . . big sneeze coming . . .

CHAPTER 8.12225

Plan Bro!

It's time for
Plan Bro.

Well, let me explain . . .

Humans love cool-looking things: fashion, sunglasses, muscles, fanny packs, attitude.

Humans also love XTREME things: skateboards, backflips, hopscotch, shark tanks.

And humans love distractions: shiny, colorful, new things.

Humans DON'T love lectures. They don't want to think about the end of the world. They don't want responsibility.

They want to play. They want to consume!

So, take all of this, combine it and slap it on you slimy folks, and you get this . . .

May I present to you . . .

These Lizard Bros are everything you're not. They're cool. They're hip. They're XTREME!

They don't have a care in the world!

They're too busy being awesome!

But how does this help us get humans to listen to our plan to save their world?

HA ha ha! Silly lizard. First, we get people's attention by being awesome—maybe sell a few skateboards along the way . . .

THEN when you're the most popular cash cows—I mean, celebrities—in the world, we can MAYBE tell everyone about your little quest.

Yes, I'm the SUPER-famous Sparkles. Can you stop gawking and get me out of this thing?

Do you understand what I'm saying?

Parlez-vous français?

184

This just in.

SPARKLES, the LAST UNICORN, is ALIVE!

However, this is not the cuddly Sparkles we all know and love.

Seen here in this blurry photo,

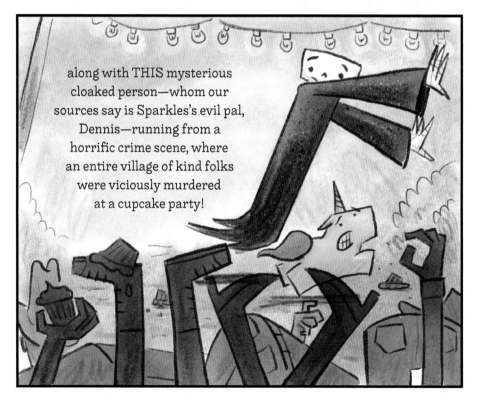

along with THIS mysterious cloaked person—whom our sources say is Sparkles's evil pal, Dennis—running from a horrific crime scene, where an entire village of kind folks were viciously murdered at a cupcake party!

It's clear that Sparkles has played us all for fools! Faking his own death to go on what can only be described as a murderous rampage!

We're going live to the street to get people's reactions.

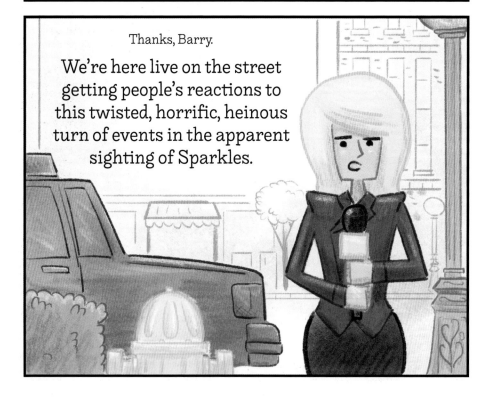

Thanks, Barry.

We're here live on the street getting people's reactions to this twisted, horrific, heinous turn of events in the apparent sighting of Sparkles.

As you can see, Barry, a real mix of emotions here ... but mostly anger. Piping-hot rage toward that phony bro Sparkles. Truly a sad day ... but mainly just an angry day.

Back to you.

There you have it, folks.

Lock your doors and hide your cupcakes. Sparkles and his evil buddy Dennis may be lurking around the corner, ready to get you next!

Have a good night.

YAY! CUPCAKES!

Maybe this isn't a good idea. We don't want to draw any more attention to ourselves.

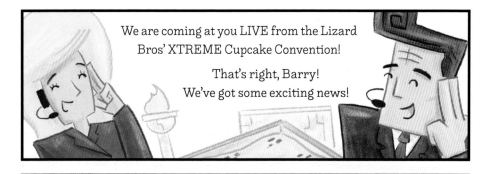

We are coming at you LIVE from the Lizard Bros' XTREME Cupcake Convention!

That's right, Barry! We've got some exciting news!

It appears that everyone's favorite XTREME lizards have caught that foul, evil, treacherous Sparkles and his weird friend...Dennis?!

Not only that—they've challenged these two outlaws to the ancient galactic lizard tradition of an XTREME obstacle course challenge.

Actually, I was about to tell you my name is D—

Shhh! Dude!

Don't worry, I'll do the paperwork this time. I'll just zap these slime wad lizards, we can grab some cupcakes, and hit the road!

I'll just take care of these doofuses and then we can break out of here.

poke, poke

Bro. Your touch of death won't work on us awesome Lizard Bros. Using our advanced alien automation, we created an advanced algorithm that renders your powers useless against us.

By harnessing the naturally occurring gravitational waves, which are then subatomically scattered across the quantum plain, your touch is therefore rendered moot.

I knew I didn't like you.

LISTEN UP! Gather round, players!

The rules of engagement are simple. Placed before you is a simple ancient galactic lizard antigravitational android puzzle. You must assemble its components in a timely manner, while making sure not to expose its mass neutrino spectrometer to any fluctuations in its magnetic field capacitor.

First one to assemble the simple device wins!

Buh?

Brodacious.

Any questions?

Uhhhhhh . . .

Done.

YAY!

YAY!

WOOHOO!

Bro! Bro! Bro!

Bro! Bro! Bro!

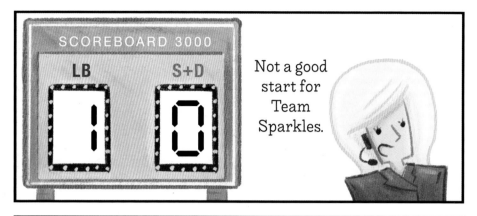

Not a good start for Team Sparkles.

And the Lizard Bros aren't afraid to let them know. Those Bros are hilarious!

Let's see if the Lizard Bros can keep this momentum up in the second round!

LISTEN UP! For the eating competition . . .

Ooooh ... The crowd is not happy about this.

Who in their right mind loves eating bugs? I knew that Dennis was weird.

SCOREBOARD 3000

LB   S+D

1   1

Things are all tied up heading into our third and FINAL stage!

GAME ON!

This is for all the marbles!

Losers will be shunned and hated forever!

Oof! I'd rather be dead! Har, har, har!

Competitors ready?

(Gamblers ready? Put one thousand dollars on the Lizard Bros.)

ON YOUR MARKS!

GET SET!

Team Sparkles is first to hit the trikes.

But the bodacious Lizard Bros are right on their tail!

They've made it to the ladders!

Wooooooow.

CHAPTER 14

Is This Paradise?

Sparkles,
you have finally
proven yourself
worthy with your
selfless acts.
You have made it.

WOW!

What a rally by Team Sparkles! This now one-man team is hot on the tail of the Lizard Bros!

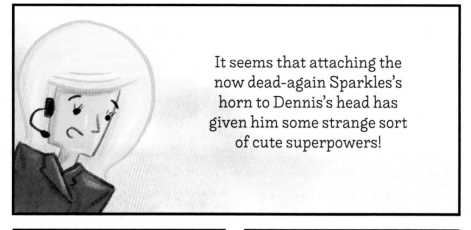

It seems that attaching the now dead-again Sparkles's horn to Dennis's head has given him some strange sort of cute superpowers!

His touch of death is now a touch of cute and cuddly!

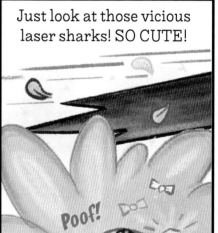

Just look at those vicious laser sharks! SO CUTE!

Poof!

WHAT DO YOU WANT FROM ME?!

For as long as I can remember, all I've ever done is try to make people laugh and smile and be their bestie! But it was never enough. Everyone always wanted more! Sparkles, gimme this. Sparkles, gimme that! AND when things got a little crazy, none of my besties were anywhere to be found. Everyone had already moved on to the newest "cool" thing.

Only one person stood by my side while the WHOLE WORLD turned their backs on me.

You're talking about me, right?

And that's this guy! A real friend. Not like a million phony friends.

CHAPTER 15
Better with Death!

Who needs 'em!

338

Funny how life works.

Y'know, I've never felt more alive.

What
EPIC
adventures
await
Death and
Sparkles?

Oh, yeah.

You've got all that paperwork to do.

Yeah.

Just a few more rounds, then.

Great minds think alike!

But
how are
everyone's
favorite
lizards
doing?

Library of Congress Cataloging-in-Publication Data available.

ISBN 978-1-7972-0635-6 [hardcover]
ISBN 978-1-7972-0636-3 [paperback]

Manufactured in China.

MIX
Paper from
responsible sources
FSC™ C136333
FSC
www.fsc.org

Design by Jay Marvel.
Typeset in YWFT Absent Grotesque.
The illustrations in this book were rendered digitally.

10 9 8 7 6 5 4 3 2 1

Chronicle Books LLC
680 Second Street
San Francisco, California 94107
www.chroniclekids.com